MYTHICAL CREATURES

TROLLS

BY THOMAS KINGSLEY TROUPE

BELLWETHER MEDIA • MINNEAPOLIS, MN

TORQUE™

Torque brims with excitement
perfect for thrill-seekers of all kinds.
Discover daring survival skills, explore
uncharted worlds, and marvel at mighty
engines and extreme sports. In *Torque* books,
anything can happen. Are you ready?

This edition first published in 2021 by Bellwether Media, Inc.

No part of this publication may be reproduced in whole or in part without written
permission of the publisher.
For information regarding permission, write to Bellwether Media, Inc.,
Attention: Permissions Department,
6012 Blue Circle Drive, Minnetonka, MN 55343.

Library of Congress Cataloging-in-Publication Data

Names: Troupe, Thomas Kingsley, author.
Title: Trolls / by Thomas Kingsley Troupe
Description: Minneapolis, MN :Bellwether Media, 2021. | Series: Torque
    Includes bibliographical references and index. | Audience: Ages 7-12 |
    Audience: Grades 4-6 | Summary: "Engaging images accompany information
    about trolls. The combination of high-interest subject matter and light
    text is intended for students in grades 3 through 7"-Provided by
    publisher.
Identifiers: LCCN 2020014859 (print) | LCCN 2020014860 (ebook) | ISBN
    9781644872772 | ISBN 9781681037400 (ebook)
Subjects: LCSH: Trolls–Juvenile literature.Classification: LCC GR555 .K49 2021 (print) |
LCC GR555 (ebook) | DDC398/.45–dc23
LC record available at https://lccn.loc.gov/2020014859
LC ebook record available at https://lccn.loc.gov/2020014860

Editor: Rebecca Sabelko   Designer: Josh Brink

Printed in the United States of America, North Mankato, MN.

TABLE OF
CONTENTS

THE LEGEND OF TROLLS

The moon shines upon the quiet forest. Suddenly, you hear a roar. A boulder flies above your head and snaps a tree in half. You hold your torch in front of you.

Through the darkness, you see an ugly face. The troll drops the old bone it was chewing on. Now it wants to eat you!

Trolls have been a part of Nordic **myths** and **folklore** for centuries. **Norse** myths often tell of mountain and forest trolls. These mythical creatures are similar to Norse giants. They often live alone.

Mountain and forest trolls are known for being strong and dangerous. They are usually slow and dumb.

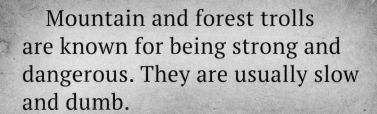

Troll Origin

Iceland

Sweden

Norway

Denmark

Europe

Norse countries =

Other trolls live with
their families in caves. In many
stories, they hide treasures in
their underground homes.

Cave trolls are mysterious
and tend to cause trouble.
They are small and have short
arms and legs. These creatures
are ugly and often have
slimy skin.

HEADS UP

In some tales, trolls
have up to nine heads!

TROLLS THROUGH TIME

Historians do not know how long troll tales have been around. During the **Viking Age**, stories of trolls were told through **oral tradition**. Trolls were described as huge monsters who fought Norse gods.

Neanderthals were related to early humans. They may have lived alongside people. They had large brows and giant jaws. Some believe they **inspired** troll stories.

Neanderthal
skull

One of the first mentions of trolls in writing was in the 1220s. In Snorri Sturluson's *The Prose Edda*, a troll woman describes herself as dangerous and powerful.

As the **Middle Ages** continued, trolls became even more dangerous. Many Christians believed trolls were evil. The creatures were linked to darkness. They turned to stone when touched by sunlight.

DAYLIGHT DOOM

Not all trolls turn to stone in the sun. In some stories, they explode in sunlight!

Hvítserkur, a rock said to be a transformed troll in Icelandic folklore

Similar Creatures

golems

Sasquatch

giants

dwarves

ogres

goblins

Around the same time, trolls took on another meaning. Many people believed trolls were like witches who practiced dark magic. They were also believed to be black warriors. They helped **pagans** fight Christians.

In some tales, these creatures magically changed their looks. They became beautiful to trick humans.

troll pillar in Lund Cathedral, Sweden

Troll Timeline

Around 793 CE:
The beginning of the Viking Age and Norse oral tradition which includes troll tales

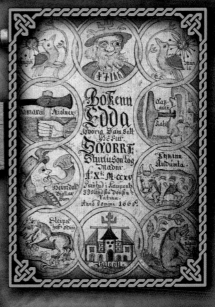

1220s:
Snorri Sturluson's *The Prose Edda* features a troll woman

1840s:
The story *Three Billy Goats Gruff* is published

Throughout the 1800s and 1900s, storytellers continued to create new tales about trolls. *Three Billy Goats Gruff* was a popular tale published in the 1840s.

In the story, three goats meet a troll who refuses to let them cross his bridge. The three goats outsmart the greedy troll and knock him into the river.

FOR WHOM THE BELL TROLLS

Trolls hate the ringing of church bells. The sound of one will make them flee in terror.

Three Billy Goats Gruff

TROLLS TODAY

Through time, trolls have continued to make their mark. In 1959, the popular troll dolls were created. The toys had cute faces and wild hair. Many had jewels on their bellies.

In 2016, *Trolls* was released. This movie included colorful, singing trolls based on the famous toys. They rescued their friends from danger!

troll doll

Media Mention

Movie: *Frozen*

Year Released: 2013

Characters: Trolls that live in the Valley of the Living Rock and help Anna after she is hurt

Powers: curl into balls that look like rocks, carry crystals that channel the Northern Lights, grow mushrooms on their backs

Trolls

Trolls continue to be dangerous creatures, too. The 2012 film based on J.R.R. Tolkien's book *The Hobbit* features trolls hungry enough to eat **dwarves**! The word "troll" is also used to describe someone who makes mean comments on the Internet.

Whether they are big and ugly or cute and colorful, trolls continue to be a favorite mythical creature!

The Hobbit:
An Unexpected Journey

GLOSSARY

dwarves—small mythical beings who are usually skilled craftspeople

folklore—the customs, beliefs, stories, and sayings of a group of people

inspired—gave someone an idea about what to do or create

Middle Ages—the period of European history from about 500 to 1500 CE

myths—ancient stories about the beliefs or history of a group of people; myths also try to explain events.

Neanderthals—ancient humans who lived 40,000 to 400,000 years ago

Norse—relating to the people of ancient Norway, Sweden, Denmark, and Iceland

oral tradition—spoken customs, ideas, or beliefs handed down from one generation to the next

pagans—people whose religious beliefs are connected with the earth and nature; in Roman times, anyone whose religion was not Christianity, Judaism, or Islam was considered pagan.

Viking Age—the period of history from around 793 to 1066 CE when pirate Norsemen occupied the area of Denmark, Norway, and Sweden

TO LEARN MORE

AT THE LIBRARY

Lawrence, Sandra, and Stuart Hill. *The Atlas of Monsters: Mythical Creatures from Around the World*. Philadelphia, Pa.: Running Press Kids, 2019.

London, Martha. *Trolls*. Minneapolis, Minn.: Pop!, 2019.

Morris, Taylor. *Bullies and Trolls: Protecting Yourself on Social Media*. New York, N.Y.: Enslow Publishing, 2019.

ON THE WEB

FACTSURFER

Factsurfer.com gives you a safe, fun way to find more information.

1. Go to www.factsurfer.com

2. Enter "trolls" into the search box and click 🔍.

3. Select your book cover to see a list of related content.

INDEX